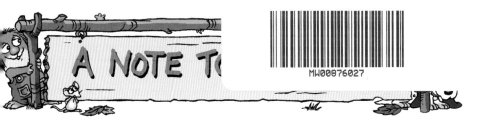

# A NOTE T[...]

ongratulations on choosing the best in educational materials
or your child. By selecting our top-quality products, you can
e assured that the concepts used in our books will reinforce
nd enhance the skills that are being taught in classrooms
ationwide.

nd what better way to get young readers excited than with
Iercer Mayer's Little Critter, a character loved by children
verywhere? Our First Readers offer simple and engaging
ories about Little Critter that children can read on their own.
ach level incorporates reading skills, colorful illustrations,
nd challenging activities.

**evel 1** – The stories are simple and use repetitive language.
lustrations are highly supportive.
**evel 2** - The stories begin to grow in complexity. Language is
ill repetitive, but it is mixed with more challenging
ocabulary.
**evel 3** - The stories are more complex. Sentences are longer
nd more varied.

o help your child make the most of this book, look at the first
w pictures in the story and discuss what is happening. Ask
our child to predict where the story is going. Then, once your
iild has read the story, have him or her review the word list
nd do the activities. This will reinforce vocabulary words
om the story and build reading comprehension.

ou are your child's first and most influential teacher. No one
iows your child the way you do. Tailor your time together to
inforce a newly acquired skill or to overcome a temporary
umbling block. Praise your child's progress and ideas, take
elight in his or her imagination, and most of all, enjoy your
me together!

Library of Congress Cataloging-in-Publication Data

Mayer, Mercer, 1943-
    Camping out / by Mercer Mayer.
        p. cm. – (First readers, skills and practice)
        Summary: When Little Critter and Gator camp out in the backyard, strange noises bother them until they
    discover that there is a harmless explanation for each one. Includes activities.
        ISBN 1-57768-806-6
        [1. Camping—Fiction. 2. Fear—Fiction. 3. Sound—Fiction] I. Title. II. Series.

    PZ7.M462 Cam 2001
    [E]—dc21                                                                                          200102659

School Specialty
Publishing

Send all inquiries to:
School Specialty Publishing
8720 Orion Place
Columbus, OH 43240-2111

Printed in the United States of America.
1-57768-806-6

 A Big Tuna Trading Company, LLC/J. R. Sansevere Book

6 7 8 9 10 11 PHXBK 11 10 09 08 07

**FIRST READERS**

Level **1**  Grades **PreK–K**

# CAMPING OUT

by Mercer Mayer

GINGHAM DOG
P R E S S

Columbus, Ohio

I like to camp out
with my friend, Gator.

*Yowl!*
What is that?

7

It is just the cat.

*Hoo! Hoo!*
What is that?

It is just an owl.

*Howl!*
What is that?

It is just the dog.

*Clank! Clank!*
What is that?

It is just a raccoon.

*Crunch! Crunch!*
What is that?

It is just Mom with
some cookies for us!

# Word Lists

Read each word in the lists below. Then, find each word in the story. Now, make up a new sentence using the word. Say your sentence out loud.

| Words I Know | Challenge Words |
|:---:|:---:|
| camp | out |
| cat | friend |
| owl | what |
| dog | just |
| Mom | raccoon |
| cookies | |

# The Letter C

Circle all the pictures that start with the same sound as the c in camp.

# Question Marks

A question asks something. A question begins with a capital letter and ends with a question mark.

Trace the question marks below. Then, try making some of your own. Circle your two best question marks.

? ? ? ? ? ?

Now, find all of the question marks in the stor

How many did you find? _____

# Noisy Animals

Draw a line from the animal to the sound it makes in the story. If you need help, look back through the story.

Yowl!

Hoo! Hoo!

Howl!

Clank! Clank!

# Oodles of Animals

Circle the animals that are in the story. Try to do this without looking at the story.

# Color Questions

Read the questions below and circle the question marks. Then, answer the questions by coloring in the boxes. The first one has been done for you.

What color is Little Critter's tent?

What is your favorite color?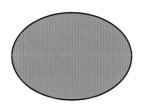

What color is your hair?

What color is your favorite shirt?

What color are your eyes?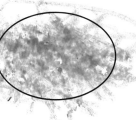

# Answer Key

## page 19
### The Letter C

## page 20
### Question Marks

How many did
you find?  __5__

## page 21
### Noisy Animals

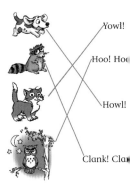

Yowl!

Hoo! Hoo

Howl!

Clank! Cla

## page 22
### Oodles of Animals

## page 23
### Color Questions

What color is Little Critter's tent?

What is your favorite color?  Answers will vary.

What color is your hair?  Answers will vary.

What color is your favorite shirt?  Answers will vary.

What color are your eyes?  Answers will vary.

We are pleased to offer these additional Little Critter® books:

# First Readers

| Level 1 | Level 2 | Level 3 |
|---------|---------|---------|
| Camping Out | Play It Safe | Harvest Time |
| No One Can Play | The Mixed-Up Morning | Christmas for Miss Kitty |
| Play Ball | A Yummy Lunch | Surprise! |
| Snow Day | Our Park | Our Friend Sam |
| Show and Tell | Field Day | Helping Mom |
| Beach Day | Grandma's Garden | My Trip to the Farm |
| Country Fair | The New Fire Truck | New Kid in Town |
| My Trip to the Zoo | A Day at Camp | Class Trip |
| Skating Day | Tiger's Birthday | Goodnight, Little Critter |
| I Love You, Little Critter! | The Little Christmas Tree | Our Tree House |

# Workbooks

| | |
|---|---|
| Math | Grades PreK, K, 1, 2 |
| Phonics | Grades PreK, K, 1, 2 |
| Reading | Grades PreK, K, 1, 2 |
| Spelling | Grades PreK, K, 1, 2 |
| Writing | Grades PreK, K, 1, 2 |
| Language Arts | Grades PreK, K, 1, 2 |

Making Children More Successful!

## FIRST READERS
### Skills and Practice

Your child's reading adventure starts here—let Little Critter® lead the way!

For over 20 years, Mercer Mayer's charming illustrations and Little Critter® character have warmed the hearts of children everywhere. Now they light up the pages of these First Readers in engaging stories that children can read on their own.

To ensure reading success, the First Readers are based on respected reading programs used in classrooms across the country. Each story uses repetition, familiar words, and sound patterns for ease in readability, while colorful illustrations provide visual cues. In addition, challenging activities and a vocabulary list reinforce reading skills.

## LITTLE CRITTER® FIRST READERS
### YOUR CHILD CAN ENJOY:

| Level 1 | Level 2 | Level 3 |
|---------|---------|---------|
| **Starting Out** **Grades PreK–K** | **Getting Stronger** **Grades K–1** | **Reading with Confidenc** **Grades 1–2** |
| Camping Out | Play It Safe | Harvest Time |
| No One Can Play | The Mixed-Up Morning | Christmas for Miss Kitty |
| Play Ball | A Yummy Lunch | Surprise! |
| Snow Day | Our Park | Our Friend Sam |
| Show and Tell | Field Day | Helping Mom |
| Beach Day | Grandma's Garden | My Trip to the Farm |
| Country Fair | The New Fire Truck | New Kid in Town |
| My Trip to the Zoo | A Day at Camp | Class Trip |
| Skating Day | Tiger's Birthday | Goodnight, Little Critter |
| We Love You, Little Critter! | The Little Christmas Tree | Our Tree House |

Guided Reading Level: D
Interest Level: PreK–2

ISBN-13: 978-1-57768-806-8

ISBN 1-57768-806-6

50395

EAN

9 781577 688068

U.S. $3.95

Can. $5.45

ISBN 1-57768-806-6

008

6 09746 11403 5

**School Specialty** **Publishing**

Visit our Web site at:
www.SchoolSpecialtyPublishing.com

# *Love*

## AND THE

# THREE LEVELS

## OF

# CONSCIOUSNESS

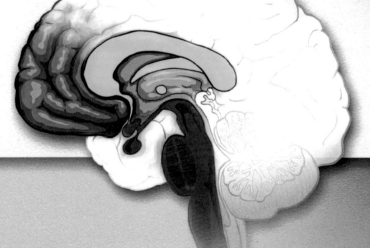

How early trauma and a fatal flaw in the human
brain combine to reduce our capacity to love and be loved

# GILBERT BATES